NUBNEB

ISBN: 978-1-947997-04-2

**Check out the first book in the Nub's Adventures series!**

Nub's Adventures: The Great Jailbreak

# Chapter One

## Back in Another Prison

"Ugghhh," Nub moaned as he cracked open his eyes. He felt like he had just woken up from a year-long nap. One by one, his memories resurfaced in his mind. Starting with the first time he got teleported away from the Nexus and into Jailbreak. Nub remembered meeting his best friend Emma, competing in a rap battle against Cole, and eventually teaming up with both of them plus all the prisoners to break free from that awful place!

Nub wiped away the goobers from his eyes and looked around to take in his surroundings. All he saw was blue and lots of it! With a jerk, he felt his floating body start moving. "Oh, here we go again!" Nub said as he prepared himself for the invisible roller coaster ride. He was back in the Nexus!

The Nexus was the core of the universe. An endless blue abyss where new players formed and existing players floated in hibernation until they're sent into another game with another mission!

Nub looked over to his right and saw tens, no, hundreds, no, THOUSANDS of other players zooming around before they teleported out of the Nexus and into a game. "I'm glad I didn't eat breakfast..." Nub groaned as the Nexus tossed him toward the swarm of players like a tumbleweed. "I wonder if any of them are Emma or Cole!" he said to himself excitedly, trying to spot his friends through the blurry mess.

**ZZZROOOOOMMM**

"HOLY GUACAMOLE!" Nub shrieked as another player zoomed by, just a few studs away from smashing him into an oblivion.

"Sorry, buddy!" the player yelled back as he continued his circuit of speedy turns, loops, and flips before teleporting away with a flash.

Within a minute, Nub had gained so

much speed that all he could see was blue and white streaks zooming by him. A vibration transferred from the inside of his head to the very core of his blocky body and it was so violent that it felt like his body was going to be completely disassembled! All Nub could hear was the whooshing of wind going past his ears as he flew with supersonic speed! Right before any more drool could fly out of Nub's flapping mouth, it came to an abrupt end.

**ZWOOP**

Either the teleportation process finally activated...or he was dead. Nub wiped the drool off his mouth and neck before looking around at his surroundings. There was nothing. Nada. It was as dark as a flashlight without power, a campfire with no flame, a cell phone with no battery, a lamp with no bulb, or a piece of toast burnt to a crisp. But then with a flash, some words appeared in front of his eyes.

*SERVER FULL. POSITION IN QUEUE: 1*

"What?" Nub mumbled to himself in confusion.

**ZWOOP**

Suddenly, he jumped to supersonic

speeds and back down to zero within fractions of a second!
"AHHHHHHHHHH!" Nub screamed, with his fists clenched and his eyes jammed shut. He was no longer floating.

"Rough day at school?" someone close by cautiously asked him.

"Uhh, yea. Sorry about that," Nub responded as he opened his eyes and relaxed his fists. He was in a bathroom facing the sink.

*Pfffft.* A fart rang out in the echoey room.The player next to him raised his eyebrows in a very judgmental arch then turned back to the mirror and continued washing his hands with a slightly worried look on his face. A whiff of someone's flatulence floated into Nub's nose causing him to choke up.

*School huh?* Nub thought to himself. *So I escaped one prison and respawned in another...* "So, uh, how do we finish this game and get into the next?" Nub asked the player next to him who was now patting his hands with a brown paper towel.

"You have to graduate of course," he replied in a monotone voice. "Four years of high school. Keep your grades up, don't make the teachers mad, survive the bullies, and don't die from the *amazing* cafeteria food," he continued with a tinge of sarcasm.

"Ah..." Nub responded, taking mental notes. "How do I know what year I'm in?"

"By the color of the band on your wrist. Every year you pass, it changes colors. Green means you're a freshman, year one. Yellow means you're a sophomore, year two. Orange means Junior, year three. And lastly, red which means you're a senior, the last year of being stuck in this awful high school."

Nub looked down at his right wrist, praying to see a red band, but instead, he was greeted with a green band. "Of course..." Nub sighed with disappointment.

"Good luck, freshie." He chuckled as he flipped up his black hoodie and walked out.

*Soooo, why did The Nexus put me in here?* Nub thought. *Is it for a mission or is it just to torture me? I wonder if Emma or Col–* Another fart rang out followed by a splash. *Okay, I need to get out of here.* He thought to himself.

Nub walked out the door while

gagging on the awful stench. Looking around, he saw empty hallways and doors leading to classrooms. Not knowing where to go, Nub took a right and started strolling through the hallway. Before he could take the next left to enter another connecting hallway, a shout echoed through the air directed at him.

"HEY, YOU!! WHAT ARE YOU DOING OUTSIDE OF CLASS???" an older woman wearing a tucked in shirt and high waisted jeans screamed at him.

"Uhhhhh." Nub turned around to face her, his heart pumping.

"DON'T 'uh' ME YOUNG MAN! WHY AREN'T YOU IN CLASS?"

"I'm sorry! I'm new here. I don't know where I'm supposed to go!"

"What do you mean?" the woman asked, starting to calm down...at least a little. "Did you skip the tutorial?"

"Umm." Nub didn't know what to say.

"These kids..." She shook her head, frustrated. "You skip the tutorial, but then complain about not knowing what to do. LOOK AT THE BACK OF YOUR BAND YOU NOOB!!" she screamed, making Nub jump.

"ALRIGHT, I'M SORRY!" Nub yelled back with panic. He lifted his wrist and looked at the band, and sure enough, there were some words on the back that said Room 212 - History 101. Nub tapped the text with his finger and like a GPS, pink, glowing arrows appeared on the floor directing him where to go.

"Now get to class... or you're going

to have a chat with the principal." The woman's face darkened. "And trust me, you don't want that." She smirked eerily.

"Okay..." Nub whimpered with his eyes round from shock.

"NOW GO!!!!" she shouted at Nub while pointing down the hall.

"YES, MA'AM! SORRY, MA'AM!" Nub yelled back as he took off down the hall following the arrows. Nub made a mental note to do his best to avoid all teachers if possible.

He arrived at a door labeled *History 101* and walked in. The room was built like a movie theater with rows of seats and a stage at the front where the professor was standing. The room was packed full, leaving only one empty seat, and sure enough, a pink arrow pointed to it directing Nub to sit there. Nub slowly made his way toward his seat trying his best not to distract his professor, and sat down to listen to the lecture.

"After that tragedy, the council of developers voted on a group of elite Robloxians to be sent throughout the universe with the sole purpose of protecting the Nexus. These guardians are now referred to as The Administrators," the professor said to the awe-inspired audience. "Now who wants to hear about *The Legend of the Wild ODer?*"

**RIIIIIIINNNGGG**

The bell signifying the class was over

barely saved the professor from an onslaught of "boos." With no time to waste, all of the students stood up and started sprinting out the door towards their next class.

"Excuse me. Pardon me. OOF! WATCH IT!" Nub shouted as he made his way towards the door. He lowered his head to check his band to see what class was next. "Science, eh? I guess it's better than math." Right before he looked up, Nub slammed into a very tall and very muscular guy who was wearing a sweat-stained tank top and athletic shorts that were WAY too short.

"HEY! Watch where you're going, Pickle Juice," Mr. Short-Shorts said aggressively.

"Well I'd love to, but I was blinded by your freakishly long, pale, giraffe legs!" Nub yelled back without thinking. "And by the way, who you callin' Pickle Juice?"

"Oh, you're a little..uh. I mean your mom is... erm," Giraffe man said, struggling to come up with a comeback. "YOU KNOW WHAT? How about we take this outside and really see how tough you are!" he challenged as he cracked his knuckles.

"Wait a second," Nub replied, having flashbacks to his successful rap battle in the prison. "Let's do this in a more civilized way." He smirked.

"Oh, yea? What are you suggesting?" the Walking Protein Shake replied curiously.

"My dude, it's called a rap battle!" Nub said, "But before I start. I need your name."

"Uhhh, I'm Tyler Taylor, but everyone calls me Tye Tye," Tyler responded with a suspicious look.

"Alright Tye Tye, I'm Nub. It's nice to meet you...and destroy you." Nub prepared a rap in his head. "Somebody, give me a beat!" he said while gesturing to the now growing crowd of spectators that were filling up the concrete hallway. A lady wearing a dark purple hoodie, jeans, and canvas shoes nodded and started hammering a simple beat on the school lockers.

"Say goodbye bye,

"To the Tye Tye,

"He gonn' die die,

"Please don't cry cry!" Nub warmed up. The crowd started "oohing" now that there was a battle.

"Your shorts so short and your legs so long,

"Call the fashion police cuz you dressin' so wrong.

"Ask Google for some food, only vegans going to show,

"You looking like a giraffe and hay is all you know!

"Your head's so hollow yet you're still so dense,

"You failed first grade, and been cheatin' ever since!" Nub ended and the crowd erupted with cheers and claps. Everyone then directed their attention to Tyler and the purple hooded girl changed up the beat a little.

"You got this Tye!" one of his hype men said while pushing him forward.

"Uhhh...err..." Tyler looked around nervously and cleared his throat.

Nub started to smile knowing he had ended this rap battle early. Unfortunately, he was right! Tyler leaped forward, grabbed Nub by the collar of his shirt, and dragged him across the hallway towards a door.

"HEY MAN! WHAT THE AVOCADO BRO?" Nub panicked as he struggled to break free.

The crowd cheered and followed them through the hallway, excited to see a real fight. Tyler dragged him out the door which led outside and threw him in the dirt.

"Square up, freshie! It's time we end this the MAN way!" Tyler snarled.

Nub lifted himself off the ground and faced Tyler who had his fists raised and his feet poised for a fight. "What was wrong with a rap battle? You scared?" Nub whimpered, looking Tyler in the eyes.

**WAAAM**

Faster than lightning, a fist smashed into Nub's right cheek, rocking his head back and knocking the breath out of him. Everything turned into a blurry mess and he could feel his heartbeat in his head. The crowd's roar echoed in his ears. He shook his head and took a deep breath to clear his vision.

"That wasn't too bad," Nub moaned while rocking back and forth.

**WHACK**

Tyler sent a fierce uppercut straight into Nub's jaw which sent him sprawling in the dirt. All of Nub's focus went to trying to stay conscious. The crowd erupted into even more cheers.

"Time to ground-pound this kid back to kindergarten!" Tyler's voice boomed as he prepared for a jump attack.

Nub opened his eyes and saw Tyler squat down and leap straight up. Tyler grabbed his leg mid-air for style points, then pointed his elbow down, aimed straight for Nub's face. Gravity did its job, and he started falling towards Nub like a meteorite crashing down on the dinosaurs.

"This is it...I die here," Nub whispered while bracing for impact. As

Tye Tye got close, Nub closed his eyes and prepared for the earth to swallow him.

**BLOOP**

The crowd went silent. Nub didn't feel a thing besides the dirt underneath him. *This is it. I'm dead. I guess it wasn't too bad. I wonder if I'm a ghos–* The eruption of cries from the crowd interrupted Nub from his thoughts and he opened his eyes to look around. He was still very alive, but the rest of the crowd was rushing back into the school through the one door. He then turned his head and saw a woman in teacher clothes standing there with her arms crossed.

"EMMA!" Nub yelled excitedly as he got up and started running at Emma to give her a hug.

"Now we're even!" Emma yelled back as her face broke into a big grin.

After their embrace, Nub asked how she did it, and where she came from.

"Well, I spawned here just a few hours ago, there was a pamphlet in my hand which explained to me that I was a teacher, and what my role was," Emma explained. "I then heard a bunch of yelling outside, came out here, and what do you know! I found you drooling on the ground with some guy about to knock your lights out," she said, chuckling.

"So where did he go?" Nub asked, awestruck.

"I sent that boy to detention! He has

to have a talk with the principal now, who, from what I've heard, is pretty scary!" Emma said, "Now let's get you cleaned up and then we can get some food."

# Chapter Two

## The Adventure Begins

"I wonder if Cole is here," Nub said while munching on his cafeteria food.

Emma started to respond, "I haven't seen–"

*"PHSTTT. Testing, testing. One, two, three. Testing, testing. PSHTTT,"* a staticky voice in Nub's head shouted, making him jump.

"Whoa, do you hear that?" Nub said to Emma, thinking he was going insane.

*"PSHT. Yeah, she can hear it. I have it set to only you two. PSHHT,"* the voice said.

"Hear what?" Emma answered with a confused look on her face.

*"PSHHT. Oh wait, I have her muted. M'bad. PSHHT,"* the voice boomed in Nub's head. *"PSSHHT. There we go. Now she can hear me. PSSHT."*

"AHHHH!" Emma screamed and covered her ears.

*"PSHHT. What, too loud? Here, gimme a second. PSHHT."*

Nub and Emma looked at each with wide eyes.

*WHAT IS GOING ON?* Nub mouthed.

*I DON'T KNOW!* Emma mouthed back, terrified.

*"Alright, I'm back! Did you miss me? How does this sound?"*

"Um...great?" Emma said to the air. Nub looked around to see if someone had planted speakers somewhere.

*"You're not going to find anything Noob, uh, I mean 'Nub,'"* the voice said. Now that it was clear, it sounded like it was from a middle-aged male sports broadcaster.

"Who are you?" Nub asked.

*"Oh, of course! I forgot to introduce myself. I'm...THE NEXUS!"* The voice boomed like thunder.

"WHAT!!??" both Nub and Emma shouted in unison.

*"Actually, I'm the voice behind the Nexus, but pretty sweet right!? Now trust me, I don't do things like this too often, but I need some help from you. Are you in?"* the Nexus asked. Nub and Emma looked at each other. Why wouldn't they accept? The Nexus is sending them on a special quest!

"I mean, I guess we're in!" Emma said. She didn't know what was going on, but who in their right mind would decline a request from the Nexus itself?

*"Perfect! So here's what's up. A group of hackers broke into our high-security storage and stole the legendary BAN HAMMER! Now as you can tell by the name, this is no ordinary hammer. With one swing, this hammer can PERMANENTLY REMOVE ANY PLAYER FROM EVER EXISTING AGAIN!"* The Nexus yelled. *"Now I*

*don't know about you, but I wouldn't want that in a hacker's hands."*

"Um, I'm sorry Mr. Nexus, but I don't think Emma and I are able to defeat a dude with some super hammer," Nub said to the voice.

*"I don't think you could either."*

Nub and Emma looked at each other uncomfortably.

The Nexus continued, *"The ban hammer requires three power gems in order to be functional and APPARENTLY, I was smart enough to hide the gems in three separate games."*

The cafeteria doors opened and more high school students started trickling in, causing Nub and Emma to lower their voices.

*"So here's the mission for you guys: Find and return the three power gems, before the hackers do!" The Nexus finished.*

"I guess that doesn't sound toooo hard. You just tell us exactly where to go, and we'll get them, right?" Nub asked.

*"Well, not exactly. Here's the thing...I know what game they're in, I just don't know where."*

"Ohhh." Emma and Nub sighed. This was going to be harder than they thought.

*"But you guys are smart, I'm sure you'll find them!" The Nexus said with enthusiasm. "The first gem is actually in the game you're in right now!"*

"Are you sure you want US doing

this?" Nub asked with wide eyes. This was an important quest, and he sure didn't want to mess it up!"

*"Absolutely! You all better not disappoint me! I have to go do..uh...other Nexus things. Just scream at me once you have found the first one!"* the voice behind The Nexus finished with a serious tone.

They both took a minute to think about what happened. The Nexus...THE NEXUS ITSELF spoke to them and gave them a mission! That's a lot of pressure!

"That was interesting..." Emma said, breaking the silence.

"Yea, The Nexus seems like an interesting...guy I guess." Nub answered, still trying to grasp what just happened.

"So where do you think the first power gem is hidden?"

"I don't know. It's a pretty big school! If you were in charge of hiding something super important and keeping it safe from most people, where would you put it?" Nub asked both Emma and himself.

"Wait...What about *who* would you put it with?" Emma answered, onto something.

"THE PRINCIPAL!" they both yelled at the same time.

# Chapter Three

## Roll War III

"So how are we going to make it in the principal's office?" Nub asked Emma. "Can you go in because you're a teacher?"

"I wish it was that easy. From what I saw, the principal's door stays locked at all times. We have to find another way in!" she answered while tapping a finger on her chin. By this point, the school cafeteria was full of hungry students. Some were in line for food while others were already chowing down on the microwaved green beans and anchovy topped bread rolls that were being served today.

"HEY! Watch where your walking!" a male student yelled out. Another kid had tripped on him and spilled food all over.

"What do you mean? You stuck your leg out to trip me, you weirdo," the fallen kid said while picking himself up and wiping some milk off of his brow.

"I'm sorry, what did you call me?" the first dude replied while picking up his own mini-carton of chocolate milk. He put his arm over the other kid, then proceeded to slowly dump the whole carton over his head.

"ALRIGHT TOUGH GUY! YOU WANNA PLAY THAT WAY? LET'S PLAY THAT WAY!" the now dripping kid yelled back after spitting milk out of his mouth. He picked up his bread roll and coiled his arm back to throw.

"STOP!" a third voice rang out. Nub looked to the left of the scene, and there was a teacher pointing at the kid holding his soon-to-be projectile bread roll.

"PUT THE BREAD ROLL DOWN....OR FACE DETENTION!" The lady shrieked so loud that the rest of the school probably heard.

The kid looked at the teacher, then looked up at his bread roll, then over to the man who wasted a good carton of chocolate milk. It was during this intimidating lunch room standoff that Nub got a sudden idea.

"Emma, I got it!" Nub whispered. "I know how to get to the principal!"

"How?" Emma whispered back, keeping her eyes on the battle.

"What if I get myself in detention!"

"WHAT? Are you crazy!?" Emma broke her stare and whispered as loud as she could without attracting attention.

"It's the only way I can get into his office without making it obvious!" Nub answered.

"Nub, how are you going to get yourself in detention?" Emma asked, shaking her head knowing this was a bad idea.

"Watch me," Nub answered with a smirk of confidence, then bolted off towards another table.

"WAIT NO!" Emma shrieked in disbelief.

Nub jumped on top of a table, which was full of random kids' food, reached down and grabbed two bread rolls, and raised them over his head. By this time everyone was looking at him. **"FOOD FIGHT!"** Nub bellowed. He then chucked one anchovy bread roll straight at the teacher's face and another one at the lactose hater! Both projectiles landed right on target and splattered fish and bread everywhere!

"RRAAAAAA!!!!!" the bread roll armed student yelled out. He jumped and threw his roll straight at the milk-waster. He now had two rolls sticking out on either side of his face!

With no time to waste, the rest of the cafeteria bursted into war cries, and fish and bread started flying everywhere! Kids were falling and slipping, and others were shouting in celebration that they'd hit their best friend or their bully! The teacher had at least ten more rolls chucked at her, so she started running around blindly and bumping into students.

"WHOA!" Nub yelled as he dodged to the right to avoid a flying clump of green beans.

He jumped off of his current table, and onto another. After scooping up and launching another lunch, he hit a kid straight in the gut, causing him to crumple to the ground from the impact of the stale pastry. "YEE HAW!" Nub yelled. He was having so much fun he forgot about the main mission! He leaped off of the table, prepared to jump the next, but someone grabbed his arm, stopping him dead in his tracks. "Uhhh." Nub looked over to his left. Standing there was a greasy, fish-covered, and well-buttered teacher with an angry smirk on her face.

"Gotcha!" she snarled. With a flash, she sent him straight to detention.

# Chapter Four

## Into the Fryer

"I promise I didn't do it!" someone begged from another room.

Just a couple of minutes ago, Nub got teleported into some type of waiting room with a line of plastic chairs pointing at a door. So far, three students have entered... and none have come out.

"Yeah, yeah. Of course, you didn't," a woman's voice rang.

"Wait, so you believe me?" the student said with hope.

"Nope. Snoogle, send him to prison like the others," the principal said.

"Yes, master. Teleporting in three seconds," a robotic voice answered.

A flash of light appeared through the one small window on the door, and that was the last time Nub saw the student.

"NEEEEXT!" the principal called.

Nub stood up and walked through the door.

"Sit down. Tell me what you did," the principal commanded. She was standing up in front of a small stool, but with her back facing away. Something was strange about her.

"Yes, ma'am," Nub said quietly as he sat down.

"MA'AM?" the principal screeched as she turned around to Nub. She quickly collected herself and muttered, "I mean, yes. Call me that."

"Uhhhh." Something was familiar with this principal, but he couldn't quite remember what. She had deathly pale skin and an eerie permanent smile.

"SHUSH!" she shrieked. "Tell me why you're here!"

"I may or may not have started a war in the cafeteria," Nub said sheepishly.

"Oh, so that was you?" the principal growled as she crept closer.

Nub gulped.

"SNOOGLE...SEND HIM TO PRISON!"

"Teleporting in three...two..." the robotic voice counted.

"WAIT! FOR WHAT!?" Nub panicked. Nub couldn't go back to the prison! He was on a mission to find the three power gems and disappointing the Nexus was not something he was going to do!

"Snoogle, cancel that command!" Nub shouted.

"Canceling that command," Snoogle answered.

"WHAT? YOU DARE BOSS MY ROBOT AROUND?" the principal screamed.

"YOU TRIED TO PUT ME IN PRISON FOR THROWING A PIECE OF

BREAD!" Nub shouted back.

"LOOK HERE, MISTER. I have to restock a prison after some TURD let all of our prisoners out," the principal said as she defended her actions.

"Well, that sounds like a personal problem!" Nub said, hoping it wasn't the same prison he escaped from.

"Wait a second..." the principal said as she leaned close to Nub's face. "You look like someone I've tased befo- OH YOU'RE THE LITTLE TURD!" she shouted and stepped back.

*Uh oh,* Nub thought. There was only one person who tased him back in the prison and he wasn't someone Nub wanted to run into again.

The principal reached her hand up to her head and pulled a wig off revealing a head full of bacon-like hair.

"Remember me?" Bacon Man snarled in a low manly voice. The principal turned out to be the lead prison guard who Nub had a bad history with!

"Ohhhhhh, no," Nub said, fearing the worst. He wrung his hands together, glancing around the room for a quick exit.

"Oh, no is right! I have something special planned JUST FOR YOU!" he snarled. "Snoogle, send him to *DEATH ROW*."

"Teleporting in 3..."

"SNOOGLE, CANCEL!" Nub panicked.

"Yes, sir," Snoogle answered.

"SNOOGLE, I said, send him to DEATH ROW!" Bacon Man shouted.

"Teleporti–"

"Snoogle, cancel, and power off!" Nub said.

"Powering off."

Nub laughed smugly.

"Fine. You want to play that way?" Bacon Man reached into his back pocket and pulled out a pistol. "I'll just do it myself." He smirked and pulled the slide of the pistol back to load in a bullet.

Nub's eyes widened as he stared into the barrel of his impending doom.

"Any last words, noob?" Bacon Man asked.

"Actually, yeah. Have you seen any special gems lying around?" Nub asked. This was the only thing he could think of to save himself. He hoped The Nexus wouldn't mind.

"What?"

"The Nexus sent us on a mission to find some gems, so I was wondering if you've seen one," Nub explained.

"Uhhhh. Not that I know of," Bacon Man said with confusion as he lowered the gun. "I only got here a couple days ago. I may have accidentally sent the previous principal to prison."

"Do you mind letting me search the desk real quick?" Nub asked. "I'll be fast, then we can get back to whatever we were doing."

"Fiiiiiiine," Bacon Man groaned after a moment of silence.

Nub ran over to the desk and dug through all the drawers. Besides the usual office items, he didn't find anything special until he reached the last one.

"What is with all this toilet paper?" Nub asked Bacon Man who was standing over him, gun in hand. There were at least ten rolls of the booty cleaner inside.

"Uhhh, I don't know. I guess when you gotta go, you gotta go," Bacon Man answered, shrugging.

Nub started pulling out all the rolls. "Five...six..seven..eigh– What's this?" Nub asked when he noticed a small wooden container inside the drawer that looked like a shrunken treasure chest. On the front of it was a lock that looked a hundred years old. "Do you think you have a key for this?"

He looked through a few dozen

keys that were on his belt loop and came across one that was different from the rest. It was a large metal key that was covered in rust and it looked like it belonged to some sort of castle. "Maybe this one. I haven't been able to find a door to use it on," Bacon Man replied as he handed the key over.

Nub grabbed the key and stuck it into the chest with a click. He slowly rotated the key and the top of the chest popped open and let out a bright golden-yellow light! "There it is!" Nub exclaimed in celebration. Inside the chest was a small, yellow gem the size of a strawberry.

"GIMME THAT!" Bacon Man shouted as he dove and grabbed the gem.

"HEY!" Nub screamed. He toppled backward and tripped on the office chair. He scrambled back to his feet and turned around, then saw that he was looking straight down the barrel of a gun.

"If you want the gem, you have to take me on this quest with you," Bacon Man said with his signature evil grin.

"Uhh, didn't you just say you wanted me dead?" Nub asked with confusion.

"Yes," Bacon Man answered, still smiling.

Nub stared awkwardly, not knowing where to go from there.

*"Ayyooo Nubs! I see you and Emma got the first gem!"* The Nexus' voice rang in Nub's head, making him jump and put his hands up to his ears.

Bacon Man also put his hands to his

ears and looked around the room with fright, wondering where the voice came from.

*"Whoa, EW! What happened to you, Emma? Your hair is...uh...unique?"* The Nexus said with shock in his voice.

"Yea, that's not Emma," Nub said as he gave a look of disgust to Bacon Man. "This guy threatened to kill me, and now he stole the gem.

*"Alright bacon boy, listen here. If you want to survive, drop the power gem on the floor...gently,"* The Nexus said to Bacon Man.

Bacon Man looked around nervously, not knowing what was going on.

*"CAN YOU HEAR ME!? I SAID PUT THE GEM ON THE FLOOR!"*

"FINE!" Bacon Man said as he put it down, "But you have to let me go with–"

**ZWOOP**

Bacon Man disappeared with a flash.

"Uhh, where did he go?" Nub said with shock on his face.

*"Don't worry. I just teleported him back to the prison. Oh, and I might as well get the real Emma over here,"* The Nexus said.

**ZWOOP**

"WHOA!" Emma exclaimed while trying to keep her balance. "Oh my gosh, Nub! I thought you died!"

"I'm all good! Long story short, we have the first power gem!" Nub said enthusiastically while picking up the gem and handing it to Emma.

"Yes! Great job, Nub!" Emma said, admiring the glowing gem.

*"Alright, so that's one down. Now there two more gems to go! Are you guys ready to be sent to the next game?"*

Nub said, "Sure, but what game is–
"

**ZWOOP**

# Chapter Five

## Booga Booga Booga

"Nub, I'm almost CERTAIN we've been walking in a circle," Emma said with frustration as she combed her hand through her hair caught in sticky strands of spiderwebs.

They spawned in the middle of a dense jungle, and had been wandering through it for hours. Nothing but trees, bushes, and a LOT of bugs.

"No, we haven't! See, I haven't seen this stream before," Nub said in denial as he pointed to his right.

"Yes, we have! We walked by this stream about 30 minutes ago!" Emma threw her hands in the air, then wiped some sweat and dirt off her eyebrow.

"Emma, trust me. I know where I'm goin– SPPLAH!" Nub spit as he walked right into a huge spider web. He swung his arms around like a madman at a dance party hoping that there was no spider on him.

"NUB!" Emma yelled.

"WHAT? IS THERE A SPIDER ON ME???" Nub shrieked and swung his arms around even faster.

"No! Now stop swinging your arms and follow me. I'm taking over the navigator role because YOU haven't done ANYTHING!"

"Fine," Nub pouted. He dropped his arms and started following Emma as they walked along the bank of the stream.

They walked for miles with nothing but the sound of running water, chirping birds and buzzing insects.

"How are we supposed to find a gem IN A FREAKING JUNGLE!" Nub whined out loud.

"WELL NOT BY WALKING IN CIRCLES YOU NOOB!" Emma yelled back. They were both hot, sweaty, and really hungry. "Wait, what's that?" Emma said, squinting. 30 feet to the right of them was a big piece of meat that appeared to be floating in the air.

"Whaaaat?" Nub squinted and tried to get a better look. "What kind of game has steak that's just floating around?"

"I don't know, but I'm going up there to check it out," Emma answered.

They crossed to the other side of the creek and walked over to the meat. Upon closer inspection, they found out that it wasn't floating, but was actually attached to a rope that was hung over a tree.

"Who would hang a perfectly good piece of steak like this?" Emma asked, puzzled.

"Do you think it's a pinata? Maybe there's candy inside!" Nub said with excitement.

He walked over to a nearby tree and grabbed a big stick that was laying on the ground.

"Nub, what are you doing?"

"I'm about to get me some candy! That's what I'm doing!" Nub spread his feet, brought the stick back, then whacked the meat as hard as he could. Unfortunately, no candy spilled out.

"NUB! IT'S A PIECE OF STEAK...IN THE JUNGLE! This isn't a birthday party." Emma laughed while facepalming.

"It was worth a try," Nub mumbled with disappointment.

**ZWOOOF**

"AHHHH!!" Nub and Emma both screamed.

All the leaves around them started moving around and they both were swept off of their feet! Within a split second, they found themselves suspended in the air, crammed inside a tiny net.

"Ewww." Emma grimaced. The slab of meat was pressed right against her face. Who knows how long that thing had been sitting out in the sun!

**"BOOGA BOOGA! BOOGA BOOGA! BOOGA BOOGA!"** A chant started echoing through the jungle.

"Uhhh, Emma. What is a 'booga'?" Nub said with terror in his eyes.

As the chanting got louder and louder, eight people emerged from the trees. They were all wearing armor that was made out of both wood and stone, and they all had some sort of spear in their hands.

**"BOOGA BOOGA!"** their chant continued. The eight islanders surrounded the net and started slamming the ends of their spears into the ground, making a beat.

**"BOOOOOOOOGAAAAAA!!!"** one of them yelled out, ending the chant.

Nub and Emma looked at each other nervously, still hanging in the net.

"Do you think we should play dead?" Nub whispered.

One of the natives grabbed an ax that was hanging from his belt, then walked over to a tree that had a rope attached to it. He wound his arm back and swung at the rope. Nub and Emma fell through the air, and onto the ground. They landed with a thud and hurried to untangle themselves.

"What should we do now, Nub?" Emma asked. They were standing back to back with a circle of spears pointed straight at them. "Do you think they're friendly?"

"FRIENDLY?" Nub asked back with terror in his voice. "If they were friendly I don't think they'd be pointing THEIR SPEARS AT US!!!"

"Booga Booga Booga." The chanting started again and one step at a time, the armor-clad warriors started moving forward with their spears still pointed at them.

"Nuuuub, we're running out of time! Think of something!" Emma shouted over her shoulder.

"Uh...Uhhhh...errrmmm... WHAT ABOUT A PEACE OFFERING?" Nub answered.

The spears were now within a foot of their faces. Emma quickly reached into her tan bag and grabbed the yellow power gem. As the spears got even closer she took the gem and lifted it into the air above her head. With a flash, the power gem lit up and shot out a magnificent golden light throughout the jungle.

"Booooooooogaaaa..." the group murmured. Their mouths opened wide from the amazing sight. They slowly lowered their weapons and kept their eyes locked onto the gem as if in a trance. Then all at once, they crossed their right hand against their chest as a sign of respect and let out another shout.

**"BOOOOOGAAAAAA!"** The sound echoed throughout the jungle.

"Booga booga." One of the natives

with a gold bead encrusted in his helmet beckoned for Nub and Emma to follow.

Hours went by and the sun started to set as they trudged their way through the thick jungle. They came across a huge waterfall and next to it was a cave entrance that was covered by a wall of vines. The two islanders who were leading the pack went on each side of the cave door and separated the vines for the rest of the group to walk through!

"Whooooaaaa," Nub and Emma said in unison. This was no normal cave. This was an entrance to a whole nother world! It was around the size of two football fields, fully surrounded by a huge rock wall, the sky as the ceiling. Inside was an entire village! Some buildings were in the trees and others were on the ground, but there was one building that stood out. It was a ginormous temple built out of massive stone blocks and dark oak. In front of it were towering pillars supporting the roof and a stone staircase that led up to it.

As the group walked towards the mansion, the sound of a chant started getting louder and louder. **"BOOGA BOOGA!"** The sound echoed out of the building and through the village.

"Where are we going, Nub?" Emma whispered as they climbed up the stone stairs towards the building.

"I have no clue, but keep an eye out for the next power gem," Nub whispered back while looking around.

They got the top of the stairs and

looked through the entrance into the building. At the far end there was a stage, and leading up to it were dozens of benches all in rows. The benches were completely filled with other islanders who were looking towards the platform holding something that Nub and Emma couldn't quite make out.

"Oh my gosh...are we going to an ancient concert?" Nub asked with excitement.

Emma squinted and tried to get a better look at what was on the stage. "Whatever it is, it looks like we may be the star performers." Emma gulped, as they walked through the center walkway towards the stage.

"Wait, is that a person?" Nub asked over the roaring chants. As they got closer, they noticed it looked like someone was tied to a pole that was suspended horizontally over the floor.

"This doesn't look good," Emma said with worry.

All but two of the Islanders in their group separated and went to the benches, and the remaining two ushered them onto the stage. Nub and Emma looked over to the person who was tied to the pole and noticed something VERY familiar about him.

"NUB AND EMMA?" the man whispered as loudly as he could.

"COLE?" they said in unison. This was their friend who helped them escape from the prison not too long ago!

"The one and only!" Cole grumbled.

"Cole, what are you doing here?"

Emma whispered over her shoulder. The two islanders positioned them in the center of the stage with Cole right behind them.

"Oh you know, just *hanging* out," Cole joked with defeat. "What about you?"

"Kinda a long story, but basically we are on a hunt for three power gems in order to save the whole universe," Nub replied.

"Huh. That kinda reminds me of a movie..." Cole murmured, as he tried to stretch his wrists and ankles which were still tied to the pole.

Suddenly the whole crowd went quiet and a tall man began walking up the same aisle that Nub and Emma went up. He had silvery gray hair, topped with a golden crown. He was missing one eye, and in its place was a red gem. With the help of a wooden staff, he slowly made his way up the aisle and onto the stage.

"LADIES AND GENTLEMAN," he started.

"So they do speak English..." Nub whispered with confusion.

"In case you forgot, I am your humble leader, King Derrick. Today... WE GOT THE BREAD!"

The crowd erupted with cheers and boogas.

"We have been blessed with a sacrifice for the month, AND A GIFT FROM THE GODS THEMSELVES!"

The crowd started cheering more.

"So who is who?" Nub snickered

back at Cole.

"Not funny. Y'all need to get me outta here before I get turned into roast beef." Cole gulped.

King Derrick continued his speech, covering topics about how their population was growing, and preparations for winter were going well.

"Now that we got the boring stuff done, let's continue the festivities!" King Derrick shouted and gestured to Nub, Emma, and Cole.

"Wait, Mr. King Derrick, sir. Could we discuss these..uh..festivities first?" Emma whispered to the king.

"What do you mean?" The king asked.

"Well how about we do a quick

meeting in private, sir." Nub smiled, he wasn't planning on offending the king in front of everyone.

The king turned back to the crowd and said, "The festivities will begin...soon." Using the wooden staff as a crutch, the king led Nub and Emma off the platform and into a room behind the stage, leaving Cole still tied up.

"What's the matter?" King Derrick said with frustration in his voice. He was sitting in a large bamboo chair and across his desk sat Nub and Emma on smaller bamboo stools.

"Look, Your Honor. You can't go through with this sacrifice," Emma told the king.

"And why's that?" He asked as he chewed on a piece of dried meat he got from a bowl on the desk.

"Cole, who is the man you tied up, is our friend and uh..." Emma stumbled as she struggled to come up with a reason.

"The gods would be VERY unhappy if something happened to him," Nub interrupted. It may have been a lie but he had to protect his friend!

"Is that so?" King Derrick questioned as he furrowed his eyebrows.

"Yes, sir. If you killed him, I'd hate to see what they'd do to your amazing civilization." Nub answered, nodding.

"KILLED HIM?" the one-eyed king burst into laughter

Nub and Emma looked at each other not knowing if they should laugh along or not.

"That's hilarious," he said. "There's no killing going on here! We aren't THAT uncivilized."

"Well then what did you mean by saying he was a sacrifice?" Emma asked.

"Well, every month we shave the hair off of someone's head and throw it into Mt. Boom-Shakalaka, which is a volcano we have on our island. So far it has given us good luck and great harvests!" the king explained. "Since your friend had such unique black hair, we decided he would be the giver! He kept on trying to run away though, so that's why we tied him up." He smirked.

Nub took a sigh of relief.

"But if the gods don't want us to use

him, we have a list of people who would love to take his place," King Derrick continued.

"Thank you, sir." Nub bowed quickly to the king.

"Well, I will have my guards take you three to a special room to prepare for the ceremony tonight."

"What ceremony is that?" Emma asked.

"The one where you hand me that beautiful shining gem I heard about. My hunters who found you in the woods told me that the gods sent you to deliver it to me as a prize for being such a good king!" King Derrick said with a beaming smile and a glow in his ruby eye.

# Chapter Six

## An Eye For An Eye

"So what are we going to do!?" Emma shouted as she paced back in forth through the small wooden cabin.

Nub and Emma had just finished catching Cole up on everything that happened. He was a bit skeptical at first but quickly believed after he saw the gem for himself.

"Okay, so let me make sure I got this right. You guys are on a quest... FROM THE NEXUS... to find three power gems. You already have one, but now this crazy king who wanted to shave off my amazing hair thinks the gem is a gift to him?" Cole asked Nub and Emma as he ran his hands through his hair, thankful to still have it.

"Uhhhh... Yup," Nub said with a blank face.

"Well, if you got teleported here, that means there has to be a second gem somewhere," Cole said as he rubbed his forehead.

"Wait," Emma paused. "King Derrick only had one eye, right?"

"Yea..." Nub said, wondering where Emma was going with this.

"And wasn't his eye replaced by a gem? A shiny red gem?" Emma asked while waving her hands around.

Nub and Cole just looked at each other.

"I'll tell you what, I'm not going to be the person who wrestles down the king. Especially with an army of those booga people watching," Cole said with shock on his face.

"I'm with Cole on this one," Nub said, trying not to barf.

"And I doubt we can just go up to him and ask him to give us his eyeball. He's going to think we're crazy!" Cole continued.

Emma sighed with frustration.

"How about this: We go to the party or whatever, and we keep an eye out for anything shiny. I'm sure if we bring our gem near it, the power gem should start glowing," Emma suggested.

They all agreed with the plan and got ready for the night. Nub was in charge of the yellow power gem and making sure they didn't lose it while they searched.

The sun went down and the party began. This time it was outside and next to a ginormous bonfire. Nub, Emma, and Cole watched as they shaved one of the islander's heads, and sent them on an adventure to climb Mt. Boom-Shakalaka. Then it was time for the gift offering.

Nub, Emma, and Cole all joined the king on a makeshift platform in front of the bonfire, and in view of the whole crowd of at least 200 people. Emma gulped. They've been trying to look for the gem all night, but they haven't had any luck.

"Now it is time for the event that

everyone has been waiting for!" King Derrick announced as he banged his wooden staff against the floor. "Nub, please show us the gift!" the king commanded.

Nub slowly pulled out the strawberry-sized gem out of a bag and held it out into the sky. The gem sparked to life and began emitting its powerful golden light.

"Boooogaaaaaa," the audience murmured.

King Derrick held out his hand in the shape of a bowl and motioned at Nub to give him the gem. While Nub was still holding the gem in the air, he looked around trying to spot any other power gem that may be glowing, but there was nothing. He turned around and faced the king, but before dropping the gem into his hands, Nub started waving the gem around the king's face in a circular motion, hoping to see if his eye gem would glow!

"Uhhh, what are you doing?" the king whispered as Nub waved his hands around the king's face.

"Um, I'm blessing you with the light of this gem, sir," Nub lied in an attempt to buy more time.

As Nub waved the power gem around the king, his ruby eye appeared to start glowing. This had to be the power gem!

"There it is Nub!" Nub heard Cole whisper from behind him.

"Just grab it and run!" Emma whispered as well.

The last thing Nub wanted to do was take this king's ruby eyeball, but it had to be done! If he didn't get the three power gems, the Nexus and every game with it could be destroyed by the hackers!

"I'm sorry sir, but this must be done!" Nub said to the king who had a look of confusion. Nub placed his hands firmly on the kings head, but then he felt a big slap on his neck.

"No, you noob!" Cole exclaimed. "Not his eye. Look to your right!"

With his hands still on the king, Nub turned his head and saw the king's staff laying on the floor. On the head of the staff was another red gem, but this one was REALLY glowing, not just reflecting the light!

"GUARDS!!!" the king screamed as he pushed Nub's hands away.

Nub only had seconds to react

before the guards pounced on him, so in one swift movement, he reached down and grabbed the king's staff and started sprinting away, with both Emma and Cole following him!

"RUUUUN!!" Cole screamed as they ran out, off the platform and away from the bonfire.

Nub looked back and saw all 200 islanders in full pursuit right behind them!

"BOOOGA!!!" the crowd yelled. No one was going to steal something from their king and get away with it!

"NEXUS MAN, TELEPORT US!" Nub screamed at the top of his lungs. He was huffing and puffing as he navigated through the dark woods.

Nothing happened and the islanders were catching up fast!

"WE'RE GOING TO DIE!" Cole shouted as he gasped for air and jumped over a tree root. Briers were snagging at their clothes, and branches were whacking them across the face as they bolted through the jungle.

The islanders were so close that Nub could hear their breathing; a couple more seconds and they could grab them!

"NEXUS! IF YOU DON'T TELEPORT US YOU'RE NEVER GOING TO SEE THESE POWER GEMS AGAIN!"

*"AAAAAhhhhhhhh."* They heard a big yawn in their head. *"Huh? Oh, shoot, my bad, guys, just woke up,"* the Nexus finally answered.

"TELEPORT US!" Emma screamed. A hand grabbed her shoulder and yanked her to a stop!

# ZWOOOP

# Chapter Seven

## Back Where It Started

"AHHHHHHHHHHHHHH!" Nub screamed with his eyes sealed closed.

"Shut up, Nub! The teleportation is over." Emma rolled her eyes then looked around.

"Oh, my bad." Nub smiled with embarrassment.

"So where do you think we are?" Cole asked while peering out the window of the house they were in.

"Well, it appears we are in someone's apartment..." Emma said as she looked around the room. There were stacks of money on the ground, assault rifles, pistols, and all the ammo someone could ever want.

Just then, the door was thrown open.

"Yes I camp, yes I'm proud, yes I know it- WHOA." A super tall and muscular man who had a huge bag of money on his shoulder stormed in and stopped singing.

Nub, Emma, and Cole all turned and looked at him with really wide eyes.

"Cole?" the giant asked.

"Tinsel?" Cole asked back with a smile.

"WASSUP, BUDDY!!!"

They ran to each other with a big hug. Tinsel used to be prison mates with Cole before everyone escaped.

"Dude, where are we?" Cole asked.

"Still in this prison game dude. I never got teleported out so I did some exploring and found out there's a whole nother part of this game besides escaping that nasty prison; we get to rob places!"

"What!?" Nub asked, a little too excited about breaking the law.

"Yeah bro, in fact, I just finished this huge train heist," he bragged as he dropped the huge bag of cash. "They never saw it coming!"

"Nice..." Cole said slowly, practically drooling over the money bag.

"So what are you guys doing here?" Tinsel asked.

"It's a bit of a long story, but basically we're on a hunt for a really special gem," Emma explained.

"Huh. Well, you guys may just be in luck. Me and a bunch of my buddies are about to go on a huge robbing spree. We're going to hit this bank, a jewelry store, and maybe even one more place if everything goes well," Tinsel offered.

"We're in!" Nub answered without even asking Cole or Emma. "Sounds like the jewelry store is a possible option!"

"Awesome! Well, gear up. The group is meeting at the bank in... 5 minutes ago!" Tinsel pointed to the pile of equipment and weapons on the ground. "I'll meet you all in the car outside!" He grabbed a box of ammo and ran back out the door.

"Are you sure this is a good idea?" Emma asked as she strapped on a bullet-proof vest.

"Look, it's the only way we're going to find this gem. We'd be stupid to pass it up!" Cole answered. He had a rifle strapped to his back, a pistol on his side, and some grenades on his belt.

"Do you think *that* bacon hair is here?" Nub shivered with worry. All the memories of being tased and being threatened at the school came flooding back to him. He pulled the slide of his rifle to load in a round, though secretly he was praying he wouldn't have to use it.

The three exited the apartment with their loadout, and climbed into Tinsel's mini-van. With the squeal of the tires, they were off towards the bank.

"Alright, ladies and gentlemen. Today is the day. Today is the day where we finally put this plan that we've been working on for... 30 minutes... into action, and we take back what was stolen from us!" Tinsel said to the group of eight people huddled around him. It was a big enough crew to cause some damage but not too many to get in each other's way.

"Here's the plan: James and Chris are crowd control. You guys make sure the bank tellers don't press ANY buttons. This is our first heist of the day and we don't want the police alerted. Emma and Jessica, you two are in charge of placing an explosive pack onto the generator to disable the security system. Nub, Cole, and I will go into the bank vault, blow it open, and grab the goods. Then we all get outta there!" Tinsel said while pointing at some diagrams on a map.

Everybody nodded in agreement and checked their equipment.

"Alright guys, let's get this bread!" Tinsel said and everyone but Nub cheered.

"What bread? I thought it was money?" Nub asked.

Everyone stared at Nub and rolled their eyes.

"Are they like gold-coated bagels or something?" Nub asked with genuine confusion.

"It's just a saying people use. You really live up to your name sometimes." Emma laughed as she facepalmed herself.

"Alright, move out!" Tinsel said with a grin.

The group crept towards the unsuspecting bank hidden under the cover of the night. Emma and her partner, Jessica, went around to the back of the bank where the generator was located. The rest of the group stopped in front of the door.

"Alright, three...two...one...GO!" James counted right before they burst through the doors of the bank!

"Welcome to the National Bank of Jailbre– AHH!" the first bank teller screamed once he noticed that these were no normal citizens.

"EVERYBODY HANDS UP!! DON'T PRESS ANYTHING OR YOU'LL BE SENT STRAIGHT TO THE NEXUS!" Chris yelled as he pointed his gun back and forth between the two bank employees. So far, no alarms.

"Back here, guys." Tinsel motioned for Nub and Cole to follow him through some side doors in the bank. They ran down some stairs and were faced with glowing, red lasers that protected the hallway to the vault door.

"You guys ready for me to blow the charge?" Emma's voice said through a radio.

"Go for it," Tinsel replied.

**BOOM**

The whole bank shook and the lights flickered off.

"Uh sir, that explosion was bigger than we expected," Jessica announced through the radio.

"Well, fart on a biscuit. I think I switched up the explosive charges for the vault and the generator," Tinsel muttered.

Just then the bank lit up with a soft, red light from the backup generators, but the lasers stayed off.

"Alright guys, we're going to have to put twice as many charges on," Tinsel said as he opened up his backpack.

They ran through the hallway and made it to the vault. One at a time, they slapped some sticky explosives onto the vault door until there were ten of them all flashing and beeping.

"Back to the stairs, boys!" Tinsel shouted as he sprinted for cover.

"AHHHH!!" Nub screamed. He ran back so fast he slipped in the hallway and rolled the rest of the way to the stairs as Cole jumped over him.

**B-B-B-BOOOOOM**

All the charges went off at once causing the lights to flicker on and off again. Dust poured from the ceiling and bits of the wall crumbled down making it hard to see and breathe. Nub's vision blurred and wobbled from the force of the shock wave.

They stumbled their way to the bank

vault and all together tugged the vault door open enough to squeeze through. Inside, the vault was illuminated with hundreds of shiny gold bars that had to be worth MILLIONS of dollars, but no gem was found.

"I've never been so disappointed with seeing this much gold," Cole said as they stuffed their duffle bags full.

"I know right. There's not even any bread in here," Nub said with sarcasm.

"Nub..." Tinsel groaned as he rolled his eyes.

They filled up their bags and started walking towards the stairs, stumbling over bits of wall and bricks on the floor.

"Are we all clear up there?" Tinsel asked on the radio.

"No cops to be seen!" Emma replied with optimism. She wasn't planning on going to jail today!

They made their way up and out, then quickly loaded everything into their cars and drove away from the bank as fast as possible. As they were driving, a strange number popped up in Nub's vision.

*$5,000*

"Whoa, what is this?" Nub asked while he tried to swat the number away.

"That's your bounty dude! Congrats!" Tinsel said with pride.

"Congrats? Why is this a good

thing!?" Nub said as he freaked out.

"The higher the bounty, the better it means you are! Check out mine," he said as a number popped up near him.

*$987,520*

"Almost to a million!" He beamed.

"So how many days till we hit the jewelry store?" Cole asked from the back row of the car.

"Around 10...minutes." Tinsel smirked.

"WHAT!?" Nub and Cole said in unison.

They pulled up to the front of the jewelry store and hopped out of their cars.

"Sir, it looks like someone tried to rob this not too long ago," James said as he pointed to the glass windows of the jewelry store. One of them was already broken.

"Everyone, keep your eyes open then. We have no clue what's in there," Tinsel said with a grimace. He pulled the slide of his rifle to make sure he was ready for anything. "This one is going to be pretty straightforward, guys. We bust in, smash the cases, and grab as many jewels as possible. Once we break the first case, the security doors will fall and the police will be alerted. We have to make it 20 stories up this building, and then use these to make our way down," he said as he pointed to a big stack of parachutes in the van. "Put on your running shoes because we will have to jump over some lasers!"

Everyone grabbed a parachute and strapped it to their back, then walked over to the jewelry store entrance.

"Don't cut yourself," Emma warned as they crawled through the broken glass window into the jewelry store.

Once everybody got through they all positioned themselves in front of a jewelry case and awaited for Tinsel to give the command.

"Everyone smash their case in three...two..."

"EVERYBODY PUT YOUR HANDS UP!" a police officer shouted as he emerged from a stairwell at the back of the building with his gun aimed at them.

Two more officers were right behind him carrying loaded shotguns. Nub heard some wailing police sirens start; they must be a couple of blocks away.

"STUPID CAMPERS!" Tinsel yelled as he sprang into action. He jumped over two jewelry cases and wrestled the first police officer onto the ground.

"AHHHHHH!" Nub yelled as he started rushing towards the officers with his criminal companions in tow.

Tinsel managed to knock out the one police officer, but before Nub could reach the other two, they had pulled out their handcuffs and thrown a pair at Tinsel. These were no ordinary handcuffs. They only had to get close to the victim before they automatically hooked onto the criminal's hands. Along with that, they had a blue glowing center that started powering up once it captured the victim!

Nub dived into the second officer, and Cole did the same to the third one.

"Chris get these off of me! I have five seconds before it teleports me back into that prison!" Tinsel yelled with panic.

"Yes, sir!" Chris said as he ran over to Tinsel and pressed a few buttons on the handcuffs. With a clunk, they fell to the floor.

"Well, that was easy!" Nub said with excitement. All three of the knocked out police officers disappeared with a flash.

"Those three get a nice trip back to the Nexus," Cole smirked as he dusted off his hands.

The squeal of tires interrupted their

celebration. Right outside the jewelry store, eight police cars came to a halt and surrounded the building. Two officers hopped out of each car and started sprinting towards the jewelry store.

"Find some cover!" Tinsel yelled. He picked his gun off the floor and hid behind the stairwell wall.

The group scattered and ran to hide behind the counters holding the jewels.

"HOLY GUACAMOLE!" Nub shrieked. He pulled his pistol out from the holster and ran to one of the counters. He took a turn a bit too fast and caught his foot on a corner. Nub slammed to the floor and accidentally pulled the trigger of his gun.

**BANG**

Everyone ducked as the sound of shattering glass filled the room.

"WATCH YOUR FIRE, NUB!" Jessica screeched as she looked over the counter to Nub who face-planted on the floor.

Nub looked up and saw the counter next to him had been struck with the bullet, and the glass had been shattered. Within half a second even more sirens started blaring, but these came from INSIDE the jewelry store. Nub looked back toward the entrance and saw the police were just a few feet away, preparing to dive straight through the broken glass window, but right as the first cop leaped, metal panels fell from the ceiling and blocked the entrance.

**THUMP**

The police officer slammed face first into the metal wall.

"Well I'm not sure if that was on purpose, but good plan, Nub!" Tinsel laughed as he came out from the cover of the wall.

"Oh yeah, I meant to do that." Nub chuckled as he rubbed the red mark on his face and picked himself up off the ground.

"Alright guys, take as much as you can hold, and keep an eye out for any special glowing gems. Our new friends over here are collecting them." Tinsel chuckled. He aimed his rifle and shot into the closest jewelry case to open it, using Nub's new strategy.

Nub, Emma, Cole, and the rest of the crew stuffed their bags full but didn't come across any power gems.

The crew climbed up the first set of stairs and were met with a hallway full of lasers aligned across the floor.

"Oh, this isn't so bad," Nub said with relief as he jumped over each one.

"Yeah, just wait, buddy. We have 18 more floors to go," James, their other crew member, complained.

They continued on their journey up each level, and the lasers got more and more difficult. The group started to separate as some were slower than the others.

"I hope Nub hasn't gotten fried yet," Emma mumbled.

She wiped some sweat off of her forehead as she reached the end of the last level, floor 19. After what felt like hours of jumping, climbing, crawling, and timing each move correctly, the crew was exhausted. Emma leaned against a wall as she caught her breath and watched the rest of the group get through the lasers - well, all except Nub!

"What do you mean? You didn't see him?" Cole argued with Jessica who was the second to last person in the group. They all waited at the end of the last level, sweat dripping down their faces, with their bag of diamonds feeling twice as heavy. Nub was nowhere in sight!

"Look, guys. He probably got fried. We have to go before the cops find another way in," Tinsel said as he started walking towards the last set of stairs. The crew followed him up to a room that had benches, and three doors.

"Finally! I've been waiting for you guys."

"NUB!? WHAT ARE YOU DOING HERE?" Emma shouted and dropped her bag of jewels in surprise.

"Well, when you guys left me on the third level, I kinda got lost but I ended up finding this elevator," Nub said with a grin as he gestured to an elevator door.

"Are you telling me that's been there all along..." James said with tears in his eyes. Apparently, he really hated stairs.

"Weeeell, that's good to know for next time." Tinsel said and took a big breath. "But for now, let's just get out of here!"

Everyone clipped in the straps of their parachutes and secured their jewels.

"I'll meet you all at my apartment!" Tinsel yelled as he ran through the door and flipped off the roof.

"Race you there!" Cole said to Nub before sprinting through the door.

"HEY! YOU GOT A HEAD START!" Nub screamed as he followed Cole.

The doors opened and he leaped off the edge of the building without hesitation.

"AHHHH!!!!" Nub screamed as he fell through the air. The wind whipped his golden blond hair back and forth. Before the ground got too close he reached his hand back and pulled a red cord on the parachute pack. With a woof of air, the parachute deployed and gave him handles to steer with.

"Okay, okay, I got this," Nub reassured himself as he glided through the city, and weaved between buildings.

As Tinsel's apartment building came into view, Nub tried to slow himself down, but he was approaching way too fast.

"MAYDAY, MAYDAY!" Nub screamed as he started flying straight towards a nearby tree.

"Houston, we have a problem!" Cole said as he gracefully landed and looked back at Nub.

"AHHHHHHH!!" With the sound of snapping branches and a solid thump,

Nub came to an abrupt stop as he slammed into the tree and hung from his parachute.

*Cha-ching*

*$15,000*

The number reappeared in Nub's vision indicating his bounty increased.

"Well, at least I'm still alive," Nub said to himself while making a plan on how to get down.

# Chapter Eight

## The Final Heist

After freeing himself from the tree, Nub and the crew made it to Tinsel's apartment, then Jessica, James, and Chris all went their separate ways leaving Nub, Emma, Cole, and Tinsel to plan the next, and hopefully last, heist. But first, some sleep!

"Alright, so you're looking for this special gem, and we didn't find it in the bank, the jewelry store, or the train," Tinsel said while pacing the room with a mug of coffee in his hands.

"Is there any other place it could be?" Emma asked, yawning as she walked into the kitchen where the guys were planning.

It was the next morning and she was ready to finish this mission. So far they hadn't run into any hackers trying to find the gems, but who knows how long their luck would last.

"There is one other place, but it wouldn't be an easy grab and go."

"What is it?" Nub asked.

"The museum. There is a ton of valuable items, and one of them could be your gem, but it's protected by high-security glass, lasers, and motion detectors. One wrong move and the police would have the building surrounded," Tinsel answered with a grimace.

"Look, man, we gotta do it," Cole said. "This whole universe could crumble if the hackers got a hold of these gems. With one swing from that ban hammer, they can DELETE someone from the nexus TO NEVER RETURN AGAIN!" he said, waving his arms around.

"Okay, okay, fine. As long as you guys let me keep all the other loot we take!" Tinsel agreed with a grin. "Plus, I have a pretty good plan on how to break in." He smirked.

Tinsel gestured to follow him and led them out to the back of the apartment.

"Say hello to Mark!" he said as he pointed to a stolen police helicopter in his backyard.

"Hello, Mark!" Nub said and waved in that direction. "Who's Mark?" he whispered to Emma.

"Nub, it's the freakin' helicopter," she said, facepalming herself.

"Oh... Hi, Mark!" Nub waved to the helicopter again.

The crew suited up, reloaded their weapons, then hopped into the back of the helicopter.

*"This is Alpha 10-321 taking off, over,"* Tinsel said into the radio as he powered up the helicopter and rose into the sky.

*"Welcome to the official Escaped Prisoner Tour! To your right, you can see the beautiful city full of lots and lots of cash. To the left, if you look far enough out, you can see where we're probably going to be locked up tonight!"* he said in his best radio

voice.

They rose above the clouds and continued their flight to the museum. A few minutes later the museum came into sight. It was a large cement building with huge pillars in the front and the main door sandwiched by walls of thick security glass.

*"Alpha 10-321 is coming in for landing. Cole, do you have the explosives ready?"*

"Yes, sir!" Cole answered as he strapped on the backpack filled with charges.

Tinsel landed the helicopter on the museum roof, and everyone hopped out.

"Help me with these charges, Nub," Cole said as he started placing the charges in a circle on the roof.

Emma and Tinsel took cover behind the helicopter and kept a lookout for any cops.

"Alright, charges are set! Ready to blow?" Nub asked Tinsel as they ran back into cover.

"Let's be quick and stealthy guys. Do not get caught by the motion detectors!" Tinsel said in one last warning.

**BOOOOOM**

The charges went off and there was a hole in the roof big enough to climb through.

"Go, go, go!" Tinsel commanded.

Emma hooked one end of a rope to the helicopter and dropped the other side down into the hole. One by one, the team each hooked their vests onto the rope and climbed down it into the vast building.

"Whoaaa," Nub said while he looked around the museum. To the right of them was a T-Rex Skeleton, and there were trinkets and artifacts EVERYWHERE! There was even a mummy casket!

"Alright guys, split up and fill your bags, everything in here is worth big money. Just make sure to watch out for these." Tinsel motioned to an almost invisible laser that was running across the floor. "If you touch it, the cops will be here in seconds," he warned.

Everyone split up and started to stuff their bags.

"Hey Emma, have you found it yet?" Nub yelled to the other side of the building. His bag was full of gems, but none of them were glowing.

"Not yet. A lot of cool stuff though! There's a golden toilet in here!" Emma yelled back.

Nub walked over to the Egyptian section and stepped over one of the many motion detectors. There was a golden goblet with bright green emeralds all around, and next to it was the large coffin.

"What if this Egyptian king drank out of this?" Nub said to himself in awe. As he set the cup back on the shelf, a man walked straight through a wall and into the museum!

"AHHHHHHHH!!!!" Nub screamed at the top of his lungs. He fell backward, slammed into the coffin, and then fell to the floor.

"Whoa, buddy chill!" the wall-walker said.

"What is it, Nub?" Tinsel yelled from another room.

"TH-TH- THERE'S A HACKER!! He walked through the wall!" Nub screamed as he scooted back, still on the floor. He completely forgot about the motion detectors and laid his hand right on one's path.

**RIIIIIINNGG**

Alarms blared, the lights dimmed, and their cover was blown! Tinsel came sprinting towards Nub and the stranger to see what happened.

"What the heck man!" Tinsel shouted to the hacker. "You know hacking is against the Nexus' rules bro!"

"Oh shush. You know they won't be able to catch me," the hacker scoffed. "Plus, I'm an exploiter, not a hacke–"

**WOOSH**

Right before he could finish his body disappeared with a flash.

"That's what he gets for blowing our cover," Tinsel grumbled as he picked Nub off the ground. "You guys almost done? The police will be here any minute."

"We haven't found the last gem yet..." Nub said with disappointment. But right then he caught a glimmer of green glow emitting out of the toppled coffin on the floor.

"What's that?" he said while pointing to it.

"Well, let's see," Tinsel responded. He walked over to it and lifted off the lid.

Inside was a blocky man all wrapped up in cloth with his hands on his chest holding a bright green, glowing gem.

"That's it!" Nub screamed. He ran over, grabbed the power gem, and replaced it with another large diamond he found for good measure.

"ALRIGHT CREW! Back to the helicopter before–"

## BOOOM

An explosion from the roof shook the building and dust fell from the ceiling.

"We got you now!" An oh-too-familiar voice echoed into the building from the opening of the roof.

Nub looked over and saw his arch-nemesis, the Bacon Man, looking in with a deathly grin on his face.

"Hey, buddy!" Nub said with a shaky laugh.

"Oh don't 'hey buddy' me!" Bacon Man growled. "All I wanted to do was to help you with this mission. BUT NO! Who wants a bacon hair to follow you around," he said in a mocking voice.

"I mean, it was more because you tased me, not because of your bacon– "

"NAH NAH NAH! Don't give me that poopy doo doo," he yelled with anger in his eyes. "I can't help that you hate Bacon Men just because we don't look as cool as you or may not be as good as you."

"Bro, my name is Nub, I'm literally a noob..." Nub replied with a blank face.

"SHUSH! I'm finally having my moment now," Bacon Man said with frustration before carrying on his speech. "Oh, whatever. I forgot what I was going to say! You and your buddies are going to jail for a LONG LONG time!"

"Not on my watch!" Tinsel yelled. He pointed his rifle and fired three shots.

Bacon Man quickly darted his head away from the hole and evaded the bullets.

Emma ran up, out of breath. "How are we going to get out of here?"

"I have tried all the doors and they're locked from the outside," Cole said as he ran over.

"Oh no no no. I can't lose my bounty! I'm so close to 1 million!" Tinsel moaned to himself.

The group heard a metal clunk and saw that the police had dropped something in from the roof.

"Uhhh, what's that?" Nub asked.

"TEAR GAS!! They're trying to smoke us out!" Tinsel panicked.

With a bang, the canister opened up and a pale green smoke started puffing out.

Nub looked around the museum, trying to think of an escape plan, and then it hit him! "Cole, do you have any more explosive charges?" he asked.

"I mean, I have one, but it won't make it through this glass. It's way too thick."

"Trust me, I have a plan!" Nub said. They had less than a minute to escape before the gas reached them. He grabbed the explosive charge and placed it on one of the window panes.

"Follow me, guys!" Nub commanded.

The crew followed him up a set of stairs towards a vintage racing display.

"When I was digging around, I noticed they still had the keys inside," Nub exclaimed as he pointed towards to classic race cars. "Pick your ride," He said with a smirk.

"Oh, I see where you're going with this." Tinsel grinned.

They hopped into the two cars, turned them on, and revved the engine.

"This better work, Nub!" Cole yelled over the roaring engines.

The museum was filling up quickly, and it was getting harder and harder to breathe.

Nub flipped the switch on the detonator, blowing up the charge and leaving the glass panel full of cracks.

"START SHOOTING, TINSEL!" Nub screamed. He floored the accelerator and drove the car down the stairs, straight towards the damaged glass window!

"AHHHHHH!" Tinsel yelled while firing his rifle at the cracked window.

The car slammed into the window and broke straight through, sending them flying out of the museum with Cole and Emma in tow.

"YEEE HAWW!" Tinsel yelled out the car window. He made it free with his bounty!

"I'll get you one day, Nub!" An angry shout echoed from the top of the museum.

They drove back to the apartment while making sure they didn't run across any police that were patrolling the city.

"Thank you so much for the help, Tinsel! We couldn't have done this without you," Emma said with a smile as she dropped her bag of loot on the couch.

"It was my pleasure guys! I'm glad we found your gem!" he replied with a grin.

"Talking about the gem, can I see it, Nub?" Cole asked.

"Yeah, of course," Nub answered. He reached into his pocket, but it wasn't there.

"Nub?" Emma questioned.

"Uhhhh...Ummm," Nub mumbled as he frantically patted his pockets.

"NUB! IF YOU LOST IT, SO HELP

ME I WILL–"

"FOUND IT!" Nub said with relief. He pulled out the gem and lifted it into the air where it started glowing a bright green color.

"Whoooaa." Everyone admired it.

"Alright, Mr. Nexus. Beam us up!" Nub said.

# Chapter Nine

## Mission Complete… Right?

With a flash, the three heroes arrived at their final destination. They appeared to be in the center of a large, and very modern city. All the buildings were made of glass and white marble, and behind them were twelve huge marble statues standing in a circle.

"Whooaa!" Cole said as he looked around at the towering buildings.

"Where are we?" Nub asked,

equally amazed.

"If the legends are true, I believe we are on a floating island that only developers and the protectors of the Nexus are invited to," Cole answered, still in awe.

"Guys, look down there!" Emma said as she pointed down the road in front of them. There was a bright yellow arrow floating over it as if it was telling them where to go.

The group started walking towards the arrow as they admired their surroundings.

"It's strange how empty it is," Nub said.

"I know, to be honest, I was expecting some sort of celebration for bringing all the gems back," Cole added with a frown.

"Oh, don't be so shallow. I'm sure the Nexus and all the Administrators will be very grateful," Emma remarked.

They continued following the arrow as it twisted and turned through the city, but even with all the buildings and houses, not another person was out on the streets! Eventually, they made it to the front of the biggest building on the island. It was so tall that they couldn't even see the top!

Nub climbed up the large marble stairs and creaked open one of the dozen front doors. "Hello?" Nub's voice echoed through the vast lobby.

They walked inside and were greeted with a sign that asked them to sign in, but nobody was at the counter.

"So... do we just keep walking?" Cole asked as he looked around.

"I guess so," Emma answered as she followed the arrow to a wall of over a dozen elevators.

*Ding*

Immediately, an elevator opened and they walked inside. The yellow arrow shrank to the size of a cell phone, then pointed to button *419*–the highest floor.

"Well, we're in for a bit of a ride!" Nub said as he leaned up against the wall and prepared for a long elevator ride.

Suddenly, the elevator took off and started climbing at an insane rate of speed!

**ZROOOOM**

"AHHHHH! I TAKE IT BACK!" Nub screamed as he held onto the railing as the floors zipped by.

Hey! Look, there *is* someone!" Emma pointed out the glass elevator and towards the street that was now far away.

"Looks like someone is training for a marathon!" Nub laughed as he watched the man sprint through the streets.

"So who do you think the Nexus is?" Cole asked as he prepared to meet the person that has been talking in their minds for way too long.

"I don't know. A person? The original group of Developers? A robot?" Nub wondered.

"Well, we're about to find out!" Emma answered as the elevator came to a halt at the top floor.

*Ding*

The elevator doors slowly opened. "Holy guacamole!" Nub blurted out. The room looked like the command center of a space cruiser! There were rows and rows of desks that were all filled with buttons and screens, and facing away from them was a man with silver hair sitting in a desk chair and watching a screen.

"Nub, go!" Emma whispered to

Nub. They were still inside the elevator.

"Uhhhhh," Nub babbled with a mix of excitement and anxiety. He was just a few seconds away from meeting the man who ran the Nexus!

"THE DOORS ARE GOING TO CLOSE, NUB!" Emma whispered as loud as she could before pushing him out the elevator.

Right as he exited, the door closed and caught his foot before bouncing back open and making Nub stumble onto the ground.

"Oof!" Nub blurted as he caught himself. He looked up and saw that the man hadn't noticed them yet. "Y'all ready?" Nub asked Cole and Emma as he straightened his shirt.

"More ready then you are!" Cole chuckled as they walked towards the man.

"Oh, there you are!" The man turned around in his desk chair and faced Nub, Emma, and Cole with a big smile.

"H-h-hi, sir!" Nub stammered as he stuck his hand out for a handshake.

"I'm so glad you all finally made it!" he said as he got up from the chair, and shook Nub's hand while squeezing Nub's shoulder with his other hand.

"It's an honor to meet you, sir!" Emma greeted him with a handshake as well.

"Aye, what's up," Cole said as he stuck his hand out for a fist pump. The man just shook Cole's fist. "Soooo, uh, you run the place?" Cole asked as he bit his cheeks, trying not to laugh.

"Ah yes! I should introduce myself, my apologies," he said with the same smile. "My name is John. But you can call me Mr. Doe!" John said with a bow. "This is one of the main offices where they–I mean I–run the Nexus!" he said, waving his hand around to show off all the buttons. In the corner of the room was a stack of over a dozen chairs.

"Do you use all of those?" Cole asked as he pointed to the chairs.

"What? Oh, I, uh, *collect* them!" John said with a laugh. "*Anyways*... I was saying, this is where I keep an eye on everything! Oh and sorry about the mess. We are in the middle of some... uh, renovations!" he finished with another smile.

"Oh, it's no problem at all! How are things going with the hacker stealing that hammer if I may ask?" Nub questioned.

"Well, because of heroes like you, it is no problem at all! That hacker is powerless without the gems!" John laughed. "Talking about the gems, may I see them?" he asked as he stuck his hand out.

"Of course!" Emma said. She reached down into her bag and pulled out a box containing the three power gems. She slowly took the top off and the whole room glowed with the bright lights from the gems.

"Magnificent..." Mr. Doe whispered as he stared into the box. He slowly reached his hand towards the box, but a noise caught everyone's attention.

*Ding*

The elevator door opened and a man came sprinting out!

"STOP!" the man yelled as he charged towards them.

"Hey, that's the guy we saw running on the streets!" Nub whispered to Cole.

Nub looked back at Mr. Doe and noticed he was no longer smiling.

"DON'T GIVE HIM THE GEMS!" the man yelled as he continued sprinting towards them.

Time froze for Emma. Should she give the gems to Mr. Doe, or should she listen to this crazy man running towards her?

"Thanks for the gems!" Mr. Doe

snarled with an evil grin. Right before the man dived towards him, Mr. Doe snatched the box of gems from Emma's hands and teleported away with a flash!

"AHHHH!" the diving man yelled as he crashed into one of the desks.

Nobody had any clue what happened. They stood frozen, watching with wide eyes, as he picked himself off the floor.

"Who are you?" Nub gulped.

The man coughed. "My name is Dr. Evan Ferb, one of the twelve original developers," he answered as he looked at them and took a deep breath.

"And who was that guy?" Cole asked.

"That, my friend, was John Doe. He is not the Nexus; in fact, he is the most notorious hacker."

Nub, Emma, and Cole all looked at each other. They'd messed up big time. They had just handed the three most powerful gems... to the hacker himself.

*To be continued...*

# Acknowledgments

Huge thank you to my family for their continued support of my entrepreneurial escapades.

My sister, Joy Chappell (@joychappellauthor) for her AMAZING editing. Check out her Roblox book series: *Roxie Noble And The Fashion Frenzy Thief* and *Roxie Noble And The Christmas Saboteur*.

Roblox for making such an amazing ecosystem that supports and grows so many creators.

And most of all, thanks to the Nub Squad for your never-ending love and support! Thanks to you, I have grown in ways that I've never thought possible and have had experiences that I'll hold onto for a lifetime. Keep an eye out for Nub's next adventure!

# NubNeb

Make sure to check out my YouTube channel called NubNeb! I post hilarious family-friendly Roblox videos!

www.Youtube.com/NubNeb

# Leave A Review

If you enjoyed Nub's Adventures: The Race Against Hackers, make sure to leave a 5-star review on Amazon!

# Stay Updated

To stay updated on the Nub's Adventures series, head over to: www.NubNeb.com/books